Witchety Sticks
and the Magic Buttons

Dedicated to
Thea - love Helen

SIMON AND SCHUSTER
First published in Great Britain in 2010
by Simon and Schuster UK Ltd
1st Floor, 222 Gray's Inn Road, London, WC1X 8HB
A CBS Company

Text and illustrations copyright © 2010 Helen Stephens

A CIP catalogue record for this book is available
from the British Library upon request

ISBN: 978 1 41691 107 4 (PB)

Printed in China

1 3 5 7 9 10 8 6 4 2

Witchety Sticks
nd the Magic Buttons

Helen Stephens

SIMON AND SCHUSTER
London · New York · Sydney

This is a muddly~wuddly witch called Witchety Sticks.

And this is her friend, Woo.

Witchety Sticks is no ordinary witch – oh, no!

She lives in a ramshackle shed
in a very tall tree and she keeps
magic buttons in her pockets.

One day, Witchety Sticks woke up in her wonky wooden bed. She wiggled her toes, stretched her fingers and pulled on her woolly socks.

"Time for a getting
dressed button!" she said.

Magic button,

witchety-woo.

Time to get dressed into something new!

Up popped a pair
of purple pantaloons.

"Perfect!" said Witchety Sticks.

She popped on her pantaloons
and set off to find Woo.

"Good morning, Woo!" said Witchety Sticks. "Are you hungry? It's time for a breakfast button!"

Magic button, bish-bash-bam.
Let's have breakfast —
eggs and ham!

Up popped a chicken. It flapped its wings and
started laying eggs here, there and everywhere.
"Witchety~wow!" cried Witchety Sticks.

What a mess!
It was time for a spring clean button.

Magic button, alacazam.

Let's make everything spick and span!

Up sprang two mops and buckets,
three feather dusters, four
soapy sponges and a pair of
washing~up gloves!

Quickly they got to work, dusting the dark corners, washing the dishes and scrubbing the floor. Then it was time for rub~a~dub~dubbing. Even Woo was dipped in the soap suds!

Before long, everything was hung out to dry.
Then the magic ran out. The buckets, the
dusters and the washing-up gloves vanished.

Everything was calm.

Until . . .

. . . suddenly a big gust of wind
whistled through Muddly Woods
and swept all the laundry into
the treetops and the bushes.
"Oh dear!" said Witchety Sticks.
"What a muddle and a mess!"
Quickly, Witchety Sticks and
Woo untangled everything.

Then, *sniff sniff*, they heard a little noise coming from under a pair of Witchety Sticks' old gardening trousers.
It sounded like someone was crying.

"Hello," whispered Witchety Sticks in her kindest voice.
"Are you alright in there?"

There was a bit of rustling.

Then out stepped a

very wet,

very upset

Littlepotomus.

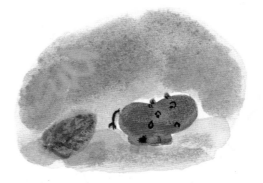

"I'm lost," he sobbed. "I was, *sniff,* eating my breakfast with my Mamapotomus and my Papapotomus when our house got dipped in the washing tub and hung out to dry. Then a big gust of wind got me and now I can't find my house!"

"Don't worry," said Witchety Sticks, "I'll find your house. What does it look like?"
"It's stripy," sobbed Littlepotomus.
"Stripy?" said Witchety Sticks, and she searched in her pocket for a suitable button.

Magic button, witchety-wows.

Bring Littlepotomus a stripy house!

Up popped a stripy sock!
"Is this it?" asked
Witchety Sticks.

"No," sniffed Littlepotomus,
"My house is stripy and round!"

"Round?" said Witchety Sticks, and she searched
through her pockets for just the right button.

Magic button, witchety-wows.

Bring Littlepotomus
a stripy round house!

Up popped a stripy
round hat!
"Is this it?" asked
Witchety Sticks.

"No," sniffed Littlepotomus, wiping his tears.
"My house is stripy and round and it has a
lovely yellow roof."

"Oh dear," sighed Witchety Sticks. Her magic just wasn't going right today. "I'll give it one last try."

Magic button, witchety-wows.
Make Littlepotomus the perfect round house!

Up sprang a magic telescope!

"I can't live in a telescope," wailed Littlepotomus, "Now I'll never find my house!"

But Witchety Sticks had an idea.

She held the magic telescope up to her eye.

It twinkled, and shone, and spun round and round until she felt dizzy!

Then she peered through the glass to see where the magic was pointing. She smiled, "Take a look, Littlepotomus!"

"That's it! That's it!" shouted Littlepotomus.

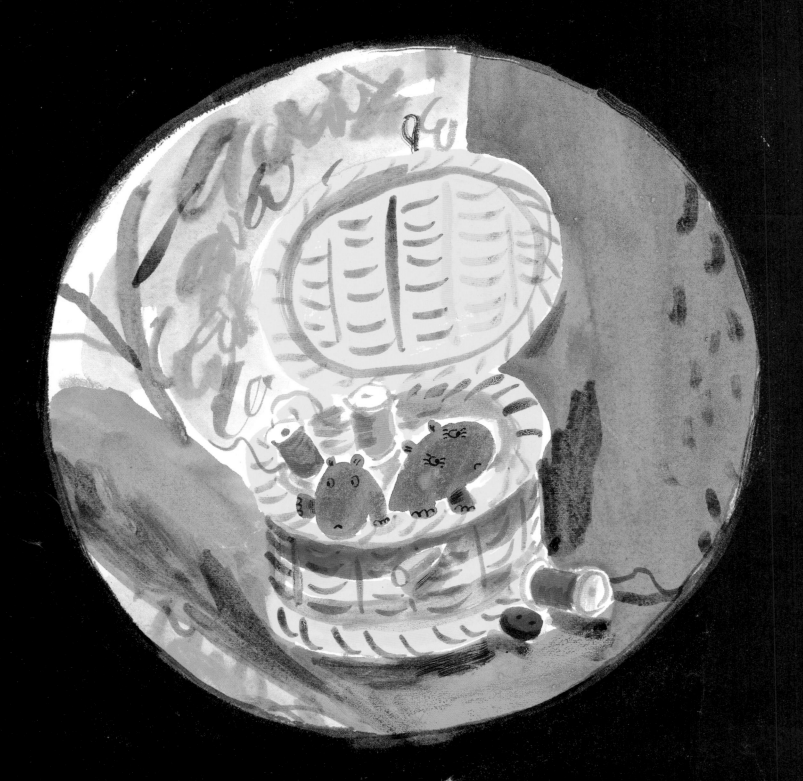

"My stripy round house with a yellow roof and,
look, my Mamapotomus and my Papapotomus too!"

"You live in my sewing box with the thimbles and threads!" cried Witchety Sticks happily, and she gave Littlepotomus a kiss on his tiny-potomus nose.

Witchety Sticks put the sewing box safely back on its usual shelf. Mamapotomus and Papapotomus gave Littlepotomus a big hug.

Then Mamapotomus made a plate of pickled~ lily sandwiches, Papapotomus poured everyone a thimble of his bubbly bluebell brew, and everyone had a very special tea.

"All we need now is a washing-up button!"
said Witchety Sticks.
"Don't you think we've had enough magic
for one day?" yawned Woo.

For once, Witchety Sticks had to agree, so she
popped the button in her pocket for another day!